FIC   Hays, Wilma Pitchford.
HAY   Little Yellow Fur.

41A1089

DATE			
NOV 1 5	JAN. 17		
DEC 2			
DEC 2			
DEC 3			
DEC 2 0			
FEB 2 9			
MAR 2 9			
MAR 3 1			
APR 1 5			
DEC 1 0 1975			
NOV 1 9			

About the book

"Play close to the house, Susanna," her mother warned. "South Dakota is wild country."

Susanna and her parents were homesteaders. They had come to live on free public land near the Rosebud Indian reservation. The Indians often rode by on their ponies. Sometimes they stopped to admire Susanna's blonde hair and look at her great dog, Terk. "Little Yellow Fur" they called her. Terk was "Dog-big-as-a-pony."

Susanna's mother was afraid the Indians would steal Susanna to live with them. But Susanna knew the Indians were her friends. She was sure that some day Mother too would learn to like the Indians.

Little Yellow Fur is a true story, based on Wilma Pitchford Hays' own childhood in South Dakota. It gives a fresh and unusual picture of growing up in the West, learning about Indian life at first hand.

LITTLE
YELLOW FUR

by

Wilma Pitchford Hays

ILLUSTRATED BY RICHARD CUFFARI

14-391

Coward, McCann & Geoghegan, Inc.
New York

For Georgia and Phil

Author's Note

When I was very young, my family homesteaded near the Rosebud Indian Reservation. With a child's trust and love of adventure, I soon made friends with the Indians. They often took me to their village, which worried my mother. I learned to speak Sioux (an ability I have since lost). The Indian women made a Sioux dress and moccasins for me.

I was only six when we left the homestead in South Dakota, but I remember many things: the day my mother pushed the table against the door when we heard the whoops of the Indian men on their ponies; the morning I met two timber wolves down by the creek. Thinking they were dogs, I approached them. They stood undecided, then slunk off into the cherry thicket.

I remember my wonderful watchdog, Terk, who was afraid of nothing except snakes. I was taught to avoid rattlers but played with a big pet bull snake which one of our hired men kept in a wagon box. In drought, when our wells and small creek went dry, snakes filled the few potholes in the creek bed, so that we could not use the water.

Then my father would hitch horses to the wagon and we'd drive to the White River. He'd back the wagon into the river. With a bucket, he dipped into the current and filled two large barrels with water.

At the time, I thought it was fun. Today I understand a little better why my mother wished to return to the pleasant town house we had left to go homesteading.

W. P. H.

Chapter 1
Homesteading in 1913

"Play close to the house,"
her mother warned Susanna.
"South Dakota is wild country.
Not like the town where we used to live."
Susanna sat on the steps of the sod house,
making a castle from wet clay.
She had heard wolves howl in the night.
She had been afraid, like Mama.
But Papa said wolves
would not come to the house.

She and her mother and father
were homesteaders.
They had settled on free public land
near the Rosebud Indian Reservation.
Papa liked it here.
Susanna liked whatever Papa liked.
But Mama was lonely so far from friends.
Susanna thought the Indians
might become good friends.
They often rode by on their ponies.
They always waved to her.
Often they stopped and talked to Papa.

Now she heard the sound of horses' hooves.
She stood up.
Many ponies were coming, running.
Indian men were riding them.
Her mother ran out the door.
She took Susanna's arm and pulled her
into the house.
Then Mama pushed
the kitchen table against the door.
She piled chairs on top of the table
to keep the Indians out.
The men stopped their ponies in the yard.

They whooped and laughed.
Sometimes they sounded angry.
Mama stood with her back pressed against
the table.
She was trembling.
Susanna's heart beat fast.
She looked out the window.
"The Indians are watering their ponies
at the windmill tank," she said.
"Maybe they won't come to the house."
But an Indian knocked at the door.

He shouted, "Drink of water!"
Papa had told Susanna that some Indians
knew a few English words.
Papa could talk to them in Sioux language.
But Mama could not.
She called, "There's a dipper at the tank."
The Indian did not go away.
Other young braves came to the door.
They pushed on it.
They laughed
as if they knew Mama was afraid.

Susanna went to the window.
There, looking at her,
were three Indian faces.
The young braves waved.
They spoke in Sioux.
Susanna wished she knew what they said.
She wished they could understand her.
"Don't frighten Mama," she called.
Her mother pulled Susanna close to her.
The young Indians went to
the windmill tank.
They wrestled and shouted for a long time.
Then some older Indians rode by.
They took the young men home.

Soon Papa came from work in the far field.
Mama told him about the Indians
who pushed on the door. She said,
"I'm afraid to let Susanna play outside."
"Don't worry," Papa said.
"I know where I can buy a good watchdog."

Chapter 2
Terk and the Indian Visitors

Papa brought home a Great Dane dog.
His name was Terk.
Terk was big.
He was tawny-yellow with darker streaks.
He let Susanna put her arms
around his neck and hug him.
Terk watched Susanna when she played
in the yard.

He lay with his jaws on his paws and dozed.
Now and then he half opened his eyes
to see what she was doing.
He taught her to stay in the yard.
If she went toward the prairie, he growled.
If she went toward the creek beyond,
he growled.
If Susanna did not come back,
Terk went after her. He set his teeth
in the hem of her dress and pulled her
to the yard.

All summer, curious Indians stopped
in the yard.
The Indian men looked at
the new frame house Papa was building.
They looked at the barn. At the chickens.
At Papa's two Morgan horses.

The Indian women and children liked to look
at Terk and Susanna.
They called him Dog-big-as-a-pony.
Terk let them come close to admire Susanna.
The Indian women touched
Susanna's blond curly hair.
"Little Yellow Fur," they named her.

They felt her pretty dress.
They pointed at
the blue flowers in the cloth.
They gave her chunks of brown sugar.
"*Chahumpi ska*," they said in Sioux.
"Juice-of-the-tree."
Susanna ate it and wanted more.
"*Chahumpi ska?*" she asked.
The Indian women laughed when Susanna
said the Sioux word for sugar.
They clapped their hands.
Little Yellow Fur learned fast!
"Hey-a-hey," they cried. "Hey-a-hey!"
Susanna knew this meant "Wonderful.
You're doing fine!"
She laughed with the Indians and said,
"Hey-a-hey!"

Her mother watched
from the door of the house.
She did not know what to do.
The Indians liked Susanna too much.
And Susanna liked them.
They came almost every day to see her.
Someday they might take her
home with them.
An Indian woman went to Mama.
She held out her own happy brown-skinned
baby. Then she pointed to Susanna.
"Trade?" she asked. "Trade?"
Mama looked more frightened.
All the Indian women laughed.
Mama could not tell whether they really
wanted to trade children or
were only teasing her.
Terk was not alarmed.
He lay with his jaws on his paws.
He watched the Indians play with Susanna
until they went home.

Chapter 3
Red Cloud

Next summer Susanna had a baby brother.
He often slept outside in his carriage.
Mama told Terk to watch him.
The big dog tried to watch Susanna, too.
But she played farther and farther from
the house.
Terk could not go after her.
He could not leave the baby alone.

One day Susanna crossed the prairie
to the little creek.
She played under the wild cherry trees
along its bank.
She picked flowers.
Like Papa, she loved this wild country.
She always found some new thing to do,
some new thing to see.
It was almost dark
when she heard her mother calling.
Terk was barking, too.

She ran home.
Papa was there.
Mama was almost crying.
"There," Papa said.
He put his arm around Susanna.
"The Indians did not take her."
Susanna gave Mama a bouquet.
Buffalo peas, bluebells, and buttercups.
Her mother sniffed the flowers.
She smiled and kissed Susanna.
But she said to Papa,
"I have reason to worry.
I'm alone here all day with the children.
I know the Indians don't want us here
on land that used to be theirs.
The young men came to the tank
again today.
They talked loud and angrily."
"I'll speak to Red Cloud," Papa said.
"He's a friend of mine.
He'll ask his young braves to behave."

The next day Susanna saw Red Cloud
on his spotted pony.
He and Papa were together at the windmill.
Red Cloud was a leader of the Sioux.
He did not wear his hair loose
to his shoulders as young Indians did.
His black hair was in two long braids.

Susanna walked closer to the two men.
They were talking and did not see her.
Red Cloud's eyes were sad.
Susanna knew why. Papa had told her.
Red Cloud had fought at the Battle of
Wounded Knee twenty-five years ago.
His wife and children were killed in the
fight with the soldiers.
The Sioux still called it
"the battle of the hundred slain."
They could not forget.

And so many settlers were still afraid
of Red Cloud and the other Sioux.
Now Susanna heard Red Cloud tell Papa
why the young men were angry.
"In the buffalo days," Red Cloud said,
"we were happy here in our own country.
The prairie was full of four-legged game.
The young men hunted.
We were never hungry,
unless the winter was long
and the snow deep.

Then the *Wasichus* came.
These settlers told us they wanted
only a little land.
Enough to set a house on.
But they kept coming, like a river.
They filled the prairie.
Their guns drove the buffalo far away.
Now our young men have little to hunt.
Nothing to do.
We must live on a reservation, in a little pen.
Our eyes run with tears.
So our young men race their ponies.
They laugh
when they frighten the *Wasichus*."
Wasichus was a new word to Susanna.
When Red Cloud rode away,
she went to Papa.
"What are *Wasichus*?" she asked.
"It means all of us," Papa said.
"Settlers, homesteaders, soldiers.
Wasichus means they-are-too-many."

Chapter 4
In an Indian Village

One afternoon Susanna went to
the little creek on the prairie.
She walked far along its bank
and picked wild cherries.
She ate a sour cherry.
It made her scrunch up her face.
She heard a sound behind her and turned.
She was looking right into the face

of an old Indian.
He was eating cherries, too.
She knew that wise face.
"Red Cloud," she said.
"Little Yellow Fur!" he said.
Indian women and children came
from the bushes.
They carried skin bags of cherries.
They laughed, happy to see her.
"Come, rest," they said. "Stay with us."
Susanna was tired. She went with them.

It was a long walk to their village.
She could not keep up with the Indians.
Red Cloud lifted her to his shoulders
and carried her.
At last he put her down
in a circle of tepees.
Women bent over outdoor cookfires.
They turned roasts of rabbit and prairie hen.
The meat smelled good,
and Susanna was hungry.
The women gave her bits of roast hen,
which they called *sheo*.
They blew on the meat to cool it.
They laughed when Susanna
licked her fingers as they did.
Boys and girls gathered around and
ate with Susanna. They gave her chunks
of crusty brown bread called *aguiapi*.
They pointed to the rustling tree
she knew as cottonwood.
Waga chun they called it in Sioux.

33

After supper the boys showed her
their small bows and arrows.
Real arrows with hard tips.
A boy said, "We must shoot well,
like our fathers.
We must grow up to be good hunters
and bring home meat to feed our people."
He climbed the front leg of an old horse
as if the leg were a tree trunk.
He climbed fast, using one hand.
He held his bow and arrow in the other,
ready to shoot.

"Hey-a-hey," the children cried.
An older boy leaped on his pony.
He shot an arrow
straight through the heart of a cactus plant.
"Hey-a-hey!" his friends cried.
Susanna clapped and smiled.
He would be a good hunter.

The girls showed Susanna
beautiful dresses and moccasins.
"Made for special feast days," they said.
The skins of young buffalo, elk, or deer
had been tanned.
The skins were soft.
The women and girls had worked
picture designs.
They used dyed porcupine quills and
tiny color beads.
Susanna put her feet into
a pair of moccasins much too big for her.
The women laughed.
They promised to make moccasins to fit her.
And a Sioux dress of doeskin.
A dress a Sioux princess might wear.

The cookfires burned low.
The sun went down.
Grandmothers yawned.
Susanna was sleepy, too.
But she did not want to go into a dark tepee.
She did not want to sleep with the Indians
on buffalo robes on the ground.

She wanted to go home.
But the prairie was dark.
She did not know which way to go.
Red Cloud bent over her.
His long black braids tickled her nose.
She sneezed.
"Come, Little Yellow Fur," he said.
His spotted pony stood behind him.
Susanna hoped
he was going to take her home.
Then a dog barked.
A big bark.
It sounded like Terk.
Susanna could not be sure.
There was only a little circle of light
from the coals of the cookfires.
Terk found her and barked with joy.

Then Papa came on his horse.
Red Cloud lifted Susanna and put her
in the saddle behind her father.
She put her arms around his waist
and held tight.
She was so glad to see him.
"I'm sorry if Susanna was any trouble,"
her father said to Red Cloud.
Red Cloud spoke in the Sioux language.
She could not understand it all.
"What did he say?" Susanna asked
when she and Papa were riding home.
"Red Cloud wants you to come again,"
Papa answered. "Red Cloud said:
  'In a Sioux village
  Every door is open to a child.
  Every pot has food for a hungry boy or girl.
  Every heart loves children.
  Helchetu Aloh!' "

Susanna knew *helchetu aloh* means it-is-true.
She felt happy.
"Red Cloud is my friend," she said.
"And the Indian women are going to make me
a Sioux dress.
Moccasins, too,
like those they wear on feast days."

Chapter 5
The Indian Gifts

The next day the Indian women came
to Susanna's yard.
They asked her to stand beside
several Indian girls.
They found a girl just Susanna's size.
Now they knew what size to make her dress.
After seven days the Indian women
finished working the dress and moccasins.

They brought them to Susanna.
This time they did not stop in the yard.
They knocked at the door.
Mama opened it and stood in the doorway.
She had never invited an Indian
to come into her house.
The women smiled and held out the dress
and moccasins.
"For Little Yellow Fur," they said.
Susanna ran to the door and took
their fingers in hers.

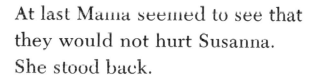

At last Mama seemed to see that
they would not hurt Susanna.
She stood back.
"Come in," she said. "Welcome."
The Indians stood in a line
around the wall of the living room.
Two grandmothers helped Susanna
put on the Sioux dress and moccasins.
They were of softest doeskin.
The colored designs were like those
she had seen in Red Cloud's village.

Susanna turned around and around.
"Like a Sioux princess," she said.
The women clapped their hands.
"Hey-a-hey!" they cried.
She smiled and said, "Hey-a-hey.
Thank you. Thank you!"
"Yes, thank you," her mother said.
"Your bead and quill work is beautiful."
Terk lay with his head on his paws.
He watched through half-open eyes.
He gave a short bark as if to say
he thought the dress was beautiful, too.
Then Mama smiled.
She clapped her hands as the Indian women did.
"Hey-a-hey," she cried.
Susanna was happy, for now, Mama knew
that the Indians were their friends.

About the author

Wilma Pitchford Hays is the author of many books for boys and girls. She particularly enjoys writing about the past, making history come alive.

LITTLE YELLOW FUR is based on her own childhood experiences, homesteading near the Rosebud Indian Reservation in South Dakota. With the skill of a born storyteller, Mrs. Hays introduces us to frontier life with its colorful features, and to the kind Indians she remembers so vividly.

Mrs. Hays lives in Venice, Florida during the winter, but spends each summer near her grandchildren in Connecticut. She is, of course, much in demand to tell stories.

About the artist

Painter and illustrator Richard Cuffari has received awards from the American Society of Graphic Arts and the Society of Illustrators. He has illustrated more than fifty books for children. He does careful research into the background of each story to make his pictures authentic in every detail.

Richard Cuffari studied at Pratt Institute. He and his wife, Phyllis, and their four children live in Brooklyn, New York.

About the Series

Boys and girls who are just beginning to read on their own will find the Break-of-Day books enjoyable and easy to read. Lively, fresh stories that are far ranging and varied in content combine with attractive illustrations. Large, clear type and simple language, but without vocabulary controls, keep the stories readable and fun.